Adapted by Lara Bergen
Based on the screenplay written by Dan Berendsen
Based on characters created by Michael Poryes and Rich Correll & Barry O'Brien
Executive Producers Michael Poryes and Steve Peterman, David Blocker
Produced by Alfred Gough and Miles Millar
Directed by Peter Chelsom

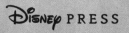 PRESS

New York

Copyright © 2009 Disney Enterprises, Inc.

All rights reserved. Published by Disney Press, an imprint of Disney Book Group. No part of this book may be reproduced or transmitted in any form or by any means, electronic or mechanical, including photocopying, recording, or by any information storage and retrieval system, without written permission from the publisher. For information address Disney Press, 114 Fifth Avenue, New York, New York 10011-5690.

Printed in the United States of America

First Edition

1 3 5 7 9 10 8 6 4 2

Library of Congress Catalog Card Number: 2008910426

ISBN 978-1-4231-1819-0

For more Disney Press fun, visit www.disneybooks.com

Visit www.disney.com/HannahMontanaMovie

Chapter 1

Pop star Hannah Montana was one of the most popular teenagers in the world. Reporters would do anything to get the inside scoop on her life.

One reporter, Oswald Granger, even snuck into Hannah's dressing room. He pretended that he was just trying to get a picture for his two daughters.

"They even wrote out some questions," Oswald said.

"Go ahead," said Hannah.

But Hannah's publicist, Vita, knew who Oswald really was. "'Country girl living her dream—beloved by millions.' That's all we've got. Now get out," she told him.

Vita was one of the few people who knew Hannah's secret: that when she wasn't singing in front of millions of people, Hannah Montana was a normal teenage girl named Miley Stewart.

Hannah Montana was so popular that she could never have a normal life. It was very important to Miley that her double life stayed a secret.

"He didn't see anything, did he?" Vita asked as soon as Oswald had gone.

"I don't think so," said Miley.

"Good," said Vita. "We want to make sure your little secret stays a secret."

Miley nodded.

Little did they know that Oswald had left his video camera behind. . . .

Chapter 2

Oswald snuck back in to get his camera, but it had been blocked. He hadn't seen Miley, but he knew Hannah had a secret. He had a story!

After that, Oswald followed Hannah everywhere. He even went to a Sweet Sixteen party for Miley's best friend, Lilly.

Miley had planned to change in her limo. She couldn't get out of the car as herself after she had gotten in as Hannah Montana. There were too many reporters.

Miley had no choice. She had to go to the party as Hannah. Miley knew Lilly wouldn't be happy.

While all the guests crowded around Hannah, Oswald walked up to Lilly.

"Is it true," he asked, "that Hannah grew up in a notable neighborhood in Nashville?"

"More like a cornfield in some place called Crowley Corners," Lilly said.

Lilly had no idea who Oswald was, or that he wanted to reveal Hannah's secret.

Chapter 3

Oswald found out that Hannah had gone to Tennessee, so he followed her there. He didn't know it, but Miley and her family were flying there for her grandma Ruby's birthday.

No one in Crowley Corners knew that Miley was also Hannah. When Miley saw Oswald snooping around at the farmer's market, she knew it meant trouble. What if he figured out her secret?

Oswald walked up to Miley and showed her a picture of Hannah.

"Do you know this girl?" he asked.

"Who doesn't know Hannah Montana? She's famous," Miley said, with a Southern accent. "I know all the Montanas-es."

Then she gave him directions to an old, empty cabin *way* outside of town.

That took care of Oswald for the moment. Then Miley had another problem.

A developer wanted to build a huge shopping mall on the Meadows in Crowley Corners. It would change the town completely.

Miley's grandma Ruby was doing everything she could to stop the plan.

That night, in fact, a fund-raising concert was taking place. A local band played, and everyone danced and sang along—even Miley.

Miley was having a great time . . . until the developer himself showed up.

"You can have a hundred of these things," the developer said, "but you're never going to raise the kind of money it's going to take to save the Meadows."

"Hey!" someone shouted. "Miley knows Hannah Montana! She could help us!"

"I guess I could give her a call," Miley said. She did not want to let down her grandma or the town.

Chapter 4

A few days later, a black limo drove up to Grandma Ruby's house. Hannah Montana had arrived. (Only Miley knew that it was really Lilly in disguise.)

"Thank you!" Miley told her when they were alone. "You're the best friend I've ever had."

Miley's friends and family had been able to keep her secret all this time. She was not very worried about one reporter.

Miley didn't know that Oswald's job was on the line. He had to get this story. The day of Hannah's concert, he was there, watching her tour bus like a hawk.

"I'm on to you," Oswald told Vita. "I've seen every person who's gotten on to that bus." He planned to catch Hannah as she got off the bus. "How's our little Hannah going to like that?" he said.

"Why don't you ask her?" Vita said. She pointed to a person with blond hair darting through the crowd.

"Somebody stop that pop star!" Oswald called. He hurried after Hannah—only to find out that it was really Miley's brother, Jackson, in a wig!

"I don't like people messing with my Hannah," Vita said.

"I don't want any more trouble out of you," Grandma Ruby added. "I won't stand for it."

So far, Grandma Ruby and Vita had been able to keep Hannah's identity a secret.

Soon Hannah's concert began. The crowd went crazy. They gave lots of money to save Crowley Meadows.

Suddenly Miley stopped singing.

"I'm sorry," she said. "I've loved being Hannah. But I don't think I can do it anymore. At least not here, not with you all."

Miley felt so close to all the people in Crowley Corners. She didn't want to pretend to be someone else with them. She decided to sing a special song she'd written, as herself, not as Hannah.

After she finished, Miley took off her wig. "Hi. It's me, Miley. Thanks for letting me live my Hannah," she said.

Miley was sure her chance to live a normal life was over now that her secret was out. Maybe her life as a pop star was over, too. Then someone shouted, "Please be Hannah. We'll keep your secret."

Miley couldn't believe it. "It's too late," she said. "I can't."

"Nobody will tell," the audience called out. Miley had helped the town, and they were going to help her, too.

"Put the wig back on!" Vita called. Miley was about to do just that, when she saw Oswald snapping pictures with his phone.

"No! Please . . ." Miley cried.

"Don't do it," Mr. Stewart said to Oswald.

"Sorry, but there's nothing on Earth that could stop me," Oswald replied. He finally had his big story!

He held up his phone and was just about to press SEND when his daughters ran up to him. They really *were* two of Hannah's biggest fans. Vita knew it, and she had them flown in.